Ready Steady Read!

Dear Parents,

Congratulations! Your child has embarked on an exciting journey – they're learning to read! As a parent, you can be there to support and cheer them along as they take their first steps.

At school, children are taught how to decode words and arrange these building blocks of language into sentences and wonderful stories.

At home, parents play a vital part in reinforcing these new-found skills. You can help your child practise their reading by providing well-written, engaging stories, which you can enjoy together.

This series – **Ready, Steady, Read!** – offers exactly that, and more. These stories support inexperienced readers by:

- gradually introducing new vocabulary
- using repetition to consolidate learning
- gradually increasing sentence length and word count
- providing texts that boost a young reader's confidence.

As each book is completed, engaging activities encourage young readers to look back at the story, while a Picture Dictionary reinforces new vocabulary. Enjoyment is the key – and reading together can be great fun for both parent and child!

Prue Goodwin
Lecturer in Literacy and Children's Books

The **Ready, Steady, Read!** series has 4 levels.
The facing page shows what you can expect to find
in the books at each level.

As your child's confidence grows, they can progress
to books from the higher levels. These will keep them
engaged and encourage new reading skills.

The levels are only meant as guides; together, you and
your child can pick the book that will be just right.

Here are some handy tips for helping children who are
ready for reading!

Give them choice – Letting children pick a book
(from the level that's right for them) makes them
feel involved.

Talk about it – Discussing the story and the
pictures helps children engage with the book.

Read it again – Repetition of favourite stories
reinforces learning.

Cheer them on! – Praise and encouragement
builds a child's confidence and the belief in their
growing ability.

LEVEL **1** For first readers

* short, straightforward sentences
* basic, fun vocabulary
* simple, easy-to-follow stories of up to 100 words
* large print and easy-to-read design

LEVEL **2** For developing readers

* longer sentences
* simple vocabulary, introducing new words
* longer stories of up to 200 words
* bold design, to capture readers' interest

LEVEL **3** For more confident readers

* longer sentences with varied structure
* wider vocabulary
* high-interest stories of up to 300 words
* smaller print for experienced readers

LEVEL **4** For able readers

* longer sentences with complex structure
* rich, exciting vocabulary
* complex stories of up to 400 words
* emphasis on text more than illustrations

Make Reading Fun!

Once you have read the story, you will find some amazing activities at the back of the book! There are Excellent Exercises for you to complete, plus a super Picture Dictionary.

But first it is time for the story . . .

Ready?

Steady?

Let's read!

Paul Bright   Matt Buckingham

Nobody Laughs at a Lion!

LITTLE TIGER PRESS
London

In the jungle, the animals were busy.

"I'm King of the Jungle," boasted
Pa Lion. "I'm the best."
"What are you best at?"
Ma Lion asked.

"Running, for a start!" he said.
And he bounded off.

Long-legged Cheetah raced right
past him. Cheetah laughed.

He laughed quietly, because nobody
laughs at a lion.

But Pa Lion heard him …

… and he was rather annoyed. "Cheetah might be better at running. But I'm better at … climbing!" he said.

With great difficulty, Pa Lion
heaved himself up onto the
lowest branch of a tree.

Monkey was
swinging high
above when he
saw Pa Lion.
Monkey sniggered
quietly, because
nobody sniggers
at a lion.

But Pa Lion
heard him.

"Monkey might be better at climbing," said Pa Lion, grumpily. "But I'm the best at … creeping!"

Pa Lion started
creeping noisily
through the grass.

Snake was slipping silently by.
When he saw Pa Lion creeping he
chuckled softly, because nobody
chuckles at a lion.

But Pa Lion heard him.

"Snake might be better at creeping,"
he huffed. "But I'm the ... strongest!"

Pa Lion pushed hard against a
small tree until, at last, it broke!
   Elephant was stomping past.
He easily knocked down any tree
in his path.

When he saw Pa Lion he trumpeted softly, because nobody trumpets at a lion.

But Pa Lion heard him.

Pa Lion was furious. "Maybe
Elephant is stronger," he said. "But
I am the best at ... Oh! I can't
think of anything!"

"It makes me want to ..."

Pa Lion's roar thundered
through the jungle.

This time, all the animals were silent.
Pa Lion really *was* the best at roaring.

And he was happy at last ...
because *nobody* laughs at
a lion!

Have you read the story? Well done!
Now it is time for more fun!

Here are some questions about the story. Ask an adult to listen to your answers, and help if you get stuck.

Top Talent

This story is about a lion who likes to be best at everything. Can you think of all the things that *you* are best at doing?

Cheeky Monkey

Now describe what Monkey is doing in this picture.

Awesome Animals

Can you name all the animals in this picture?
What is your favourite animal?

Happy Lion

Can you remember what Lion is *really* best at doing?
Are *you* good at it too?

Picture Dictionary

Can you read all of these words from the story?

boasted

cheetah

creeping

elephant

furious

lion

monkey

raced

snake

swinging

Can you think of any other words that describe these pictures — for example, what colours can you see? Why not try to spell some of these words? Ask an adult to help!

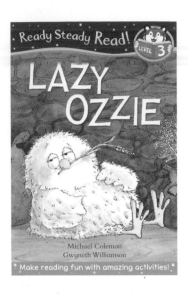

Lazy Ozzie

Lazy Ozzie is too lazy to learn how to fly. So he thinks of a brilliant plan to fool his mum into thinking he can. But will Ozzie's mum be so easily fooled . . . ?

Little Mouse and the Big Red Apple

Mouse does not want to share his big, juicy apple but he is too small to move it on his own. Can he get his friends to help and still eat it all himself?

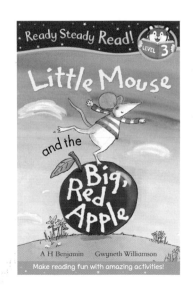

Ridiculous!

One snowy day, Shelley leaves her cosy bed to go on an adventure. But whoever heard of a tortoise out in winter . . . ?
Ridiculous!

Who's Been Eating My Porridge?

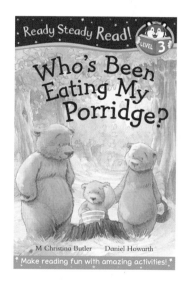

Little Bear will not eat his porridge. So his mother gives it to Old Scary Bear in the woods. Little Bear does not believe in the Scary Bear. But *someone* has been eating his porridge . . . !

For Helen, with love — P B
For Tom and Emily — M B

LITTLE TIGER PRESS, 1 The Coda Centre, 189 Munster Road, London SW6 6AW
First published in Great Britain 2005
This edition published 2013
Text copyright © Paul Bright 2005, 2013
Illustrations copyright © Matt Buckingham 2005, 2013
All rights reserved
Printed in China
978-1-84895-675-9
LTP/1800/0595/0413
2 4 6 8 10 9 7 5 3 1

Books in the Series

LEVEL 1 – For first readers

Can't You Sleep, Dotty?

Fred

My Turn!

Rosie's Special Surprise

What Bear Likes Best!

LEVEL 2 – For developing readers

Hopping Mad!

Newton

Ouch!

Where There's a Bear, There's Trouble!

The Wish Cat

LEVEL 3 – For more confident readers

Lazy Ozzie

Little Mouse and the Big Red Apple

Nobody Laughs at a Lion!

Ridiculous!

Who's Been Eating My Porridge?

LEVEL 4 – For able readers

The Biggest Baddest Wolf

Meggie Moon

Mouse, Mole and the Falling Star

The Nutty Nut Chase

Robot Dog